*Every new generation of children is enthralled by the famous stories in our Well-loved Tales series. Younger ones love to have the story read to them, and to examine each tiny detail of the full colour illustrations. Older children will enjoy the exciting stories in an easy-to-read text.*

First edition

# Thumbelina

retold for easy reading
by BERENICE DYER

illustrated by PETULA STONE

Ladybird Books Loughborough

Once there was a woman who wanted a little girl very much indeed. She went to a wise old woman and said, "I do so want a little girl, a tiny little girl."

The old woman gave her a seed
of barley.

"This is not the same sort of seed
that is planted in the fields," she
said. "This is not the same sort of
seed that is given to hens. Take it
home and plant it in a flower pot."

So the woman took it home and planted it in a flower pot. Soon it grew into a beautiful flower like a red and yellow tulip. In the middle of the flower sat a little girl. She was so tiny that she was only half as big as a thumb. The woman called her Thumbelina.

Thumbelina had half a walnut for a bed. She had violet petals for a mattress and a rose petal to cover her. In the daytime she played on the table and sang happy songs in her sweet little voice.

One night an ugly old toad came
hopping by. She stopped to look at
Thumbelina asleep in her walnut-
shell bed.

"What a pretty wife she would
make for my son!" said the toad
to herself. Quickly she picked up
the bed with Thumbelina in it and
hopped away.

The toad took the bed down to the stream and put it on a water-lily leaf.

It was a long way from the bank so
Thumbelina could not run away.

The next day the toad came back with her son. Thumbelina did not want to marry him at all. He was just as ugly as his mother.

The toad and her son took the little
walnut-shell bed back to their own
house in the marsh. They left
Thumbelina on the lily leaf while
they got the house ready for her.

The fish swimming in the stream heard the toad talking about the new wife that her son was going to have. They swam up to the leaf to look at Thumbelina. As soon as they saw her they knew that she was too pretty to marry an ugly toad and live with his mother in a marsh. There was only one way to help her. They bit the stem under the leaf until they bit it right through.

Then the leaf floated away down
the stream and Thumbelina floated
too. She floated away from the
toad and away from the toad's
son. She floated down the stream
in the sunshine. A butterfly flew
around her and Thumbelina was
happy again.

Suddenly a maybug flew down and
picked up Thumbelina. He took
her away from the leaf, away from
the butterfly and up into a tree.

"How pretty she is!" he said.

But all the other maybugs said,
"Ugh! She has only two legs. How
ugly she is!"

"Ugh! She hasn't got any feelers.
How ugly she is!"

"Ugh! She has got a tiny waist.
How ugly she is!"

So the maybug said, "Ugh! How
ugly she is!"

Then he picked her up and flew down to the ground. He put her on a daisy and he left her there.

Thumbelina made herself a little bed out of grass. All through the summer she lived by herself in the wood.

She drank the dew from the leaves
and she ate the honey from the
flowers. She listened to the birds
and she sang songs to herself.

When winter came it began to snow. Poor Thumbelina was very cold. She could find nothing to eat. She was very hungry. She came to a hole where a fieldmouse lived.

"Oh please, can you give me some food?" she cried. The fieldmouse was very sorry for poor little Thumbelina. She asked her to come in and gave her some food.

"You can live with me in my nice warm room if you like," she said. "You can clean the room for me."

So Thumbelina lived with the fieldmouse, cleaned her room, told her stories and sang her songs.

"If you marry the mole," said the fieldmouse one day, "you will live in a bigger house than mine. You must tell him your best stories and sing him your best songs when he comes."

But Thumbelina did not like the mole and did not want to marry him.

One day he dug a new tunnel to
the hole where the fieldmouse
lived.

"You can walk in my tunnel if you like," the mole said to Thumbelina, "but be careful, there is a dead bird in it."

Thumbelina was sorry for the poor
bird.

"He was a swallow and perhaps he sang to me last summer," she said to herself. "I will cover him up."

As she covered him up, she felt his heart still beating. The swallow was not dead. He was still alive but very weak.

All through the winter Thumbelina
looked after the swallow. In the
spring he was strong again.
Thumbelina made a hole in the
ceiling and he flew out.

"Goodbye. Goodbye," he said and flew away.

"Goodbye. Goodbye," cried Thumbelina.

"You must marry the mole at the
end of the summer," said the
fieldmouse. "You must make
yourself some nice new clothes
first."

At last the summer was over. The
new clothes were made.

Thumbelina stood at the door of the fieldmouse's hole to say goodbye to the sunshine. The mole's house was underground. He never saw the sun.

"Goodbye sun," she cried sadly.
She saw the swallows flying in the
sky.

"Goodbye swallows," she cried.

One swallow came down to her. It

was the swallow that she had

looked after.

"It will be cold again soon," he said. "I am flying to a country where it is warm. Climb onto my back and come with me."

So Thumbelina climbed onto the
swallow's back and they flew away.
Miles and miles and miles they flew
until they came to a warm country.

"Here we are," cried the swallow
and put Thumbelina down.

All around her were beautiful
flowers and inside each one was a
little man or a little woman just as
tiny as she was herself. They didn't
call her Thumbelina. They called

her Maia, and when she married
the little Prince of the Flower
People, they were all as happy as
she was.